This book belongs to

Super _____

Superhero Swamp

John Trent, Ph.D.

Thomas Nelson

Since 1798

NASHVILLE DALLAS MEXICO CITY RIO DE JANEIRO BEIJING

SUPERHERO SWAMP

Copyright © 2007 by Dr. John Trent

Published in Nashville, Tennessee, by Thomas Nelson, Inc.

Library of Congress Cataloging-in-Publication Data [to come]
ISBN 13: 978-1-59145-487-8
ISBN 10: 1-59145-487-5

Printed in China

07 08 09 HH 9 8 7 6 5 4 3 2 1

A Special Note from the Author

I know your kid is "super." This book is just the thing to help them see not only how valuable they are, but also the difference they can make in the lives of others. By reading this story to them, they'll learn what's really "super" about sharing and caring, seen through the lives of a swamp full of colorful "critters."

What I hope you'll do as well is take advantage of the "SuperHero Stickers" at the end of this book. When you "catch" your child doing something "super" that a hippo or alligator or frog or parrot learned to do in the book, that's your chance to make special mention of your child's act of service, caring, or sharing and present one of these colorful stickers. Affirming our child's strengths and their choices to build up and encourage others when they're young is a great way of seeing those "super" traits lived out as they grow older. So, thanks for being a "super" parent, and for reminding your child about "GMUASH!" (something you'll learn about in the pages that follow).

Blessings on you and your child!

John Trent, Ph.D.
President, The Center for StrongFamilies and StrongFamilies.com

To a "super" wife, Cindy, who has filled
the Trent "swamp" with caring and sharing
for almost three decades, and to the two
"super" daughters, Kari and Laura, whom
the Lord placed in our lives as priceless gifts.

Chapter One

It was the best swamp ever!
Mud so thick in places, even the ducks needed stilts to walk around!

Water so green, smelly, and slimy that the large crawfish invited
their friends for at least one "green tea" party a day . . . yuck!

Swarms of mosquitoes that never bit you and were so big,
they loved giving the youngest animals parasailing rides!

But it wasn't just the muck, mud, moss, and mosquitoes that made this the best swamp ever.

It was the special group of animals. There were hippos from Africa, parrots from South America . . . animals from all over the world in this southern Louisiana swamp. And not only was it animals from all over the world, it was animals who naturally didn't get along, like frogs and mosquitoes, or alligators and bunnies.

But the most special thing about the swamp was the way all the animals that lived there treated each other—like very best friends. Where else would you see wild pigs acting like taxis for entire families of raccoons who needed to cross the swamp?

Or where else did soft, fluffy bunnies help alligators brush their teeth way back where their short arms couldn't reach—without even once being snapped at?

And where else could you go every Friday night to an All-Swamp dance?! The place to go to hear everyone's favorite band play their hit singles, "Do Your Ears Hang Low? Do You Have Ears At All?" and "Who Let the Frogs Out? Croak, Croak, Croak, Croak, Croak."

Yep, it was the very best of swamps all right.

That is . . .

Until it happened!

Chapter Two

The "it" that happened was the hippo-hogging. If you've never heard of hippo-hogging, it is not a pretty sight. At the swimming pool in the middle of the best swamp ever, the bigger animals would stay in the deep end to give room for the little animals in the shallow end.

But that all changed when one hippo named Hubba hogged the shallow end of the pool—and he did so with a huge splash!

Unfortunately, Hubba's hippo-hogging started all the other hippos hogging too. So now Heidi, Holly, Howard, Herbert, Harley, Haley, Hal, Ham, Hanna, Hans, Harmony, Harold, Hidalgo, Harriett, Hayden, Health, Howie, and Heather Hippo were all hogging the entire pool!

If all the hogging weren't bad enough . . .

All of a sudden, the alligators started snapping!

When Abigail asked Alexander Alligator if he was winning at Frog Pog, he snapped, "Mind your own business!"

Then, when Abigail Alligator's mother asked her to come set the table, she snapped, "I'm busy!"

Then, Abigail's mother turned and snapped at Abigail's father as he was coming in the door ... Soon, every alligator in the swamp was snipping and snapping at everyone about everything!

But the worst teasing of all
happened when they would hang
out at the ice cream shop, stick out
their incredibly long tongues, and take a
lick out of everyone's ice cream cone—
which was sort of funny, unless it was your cone.

The very best swamp had gotten so bad that the normally nice crabs started being crabby and bossy. Every crab in the entire swamp started thinking they were the boss of everyone. They followed the other animals around everywhere, telling them, "Tie that shoe!" "Don't eat that!" "Don't even think about playing that game! We're playing this game, my way, right now!" And if you didn't do what they said, they'd pinch you!

Yes, things had gotten so bad that when all the animals showed up for Friday's All-Swamp dance, it wasn't any fun at all . . . not with all the hippo-hogging, alligator-snapping, parrot-repeating, frog-teasing, and crab-bossing going on.

It was like they had all forgotten that they were supposed to treat one another with love and respect.

Chapter Three

But there was one animal who didn't forget.

Back in the left corner of the swamp, just behind a big tree, a small, quiet voice said, "Dear God, our little swamp needs some super-big help."

And that's when something big happened.
Something . . . super.

Suddenly, from out of nowhere (actually, from the middle of a big tree that no one noticed), a super hero fell right into their midst! They could tell it was a super hero, because it had on a super hero costume with the letters G-M-U-A-S-H on its chest.

"It is me! . . . Um, I mean, it is I!" the caped creature announced.

After a long pause, one of the turtles asked, "Pardon me . . . who would 'I' be?"

"It is I," the rabbit said, *"SuperHero SuperHero–Maker!* I've come to make all of you into super heroes like me!"

And again from out of nowhere (but actually from behind his cape), the SuperHero SuperHero- Maker pulled out packages of super costumes, enough for every animal.

He started by tossing the hippos sparkling ballerina costumes! While the hippos quickly squeezed into their costumes, the rabbit announced, "Forget Hippo-hogging! From now on, you are Super-Sharers!"

Suddenly, the hippos became super at sharing with others.
In the days to come, they would start sharing at the pool again.
They would let the smaller animals have the front seats at the
movies. They would even start sharing their popcorn with their
super hero siblings (which made at least two of their hippo
parents faint on the spot).

But SuperHero SuperHero-Maker was just getting started.

Next, he handed all the snapping alligators super hero nurse outfits. "Forget all that snapping," he said. "You are now Super-Carers!" And suddenly, it seemed that everywhere you looked, there were alligators caring for others and saying nice things instead of being so snappy.

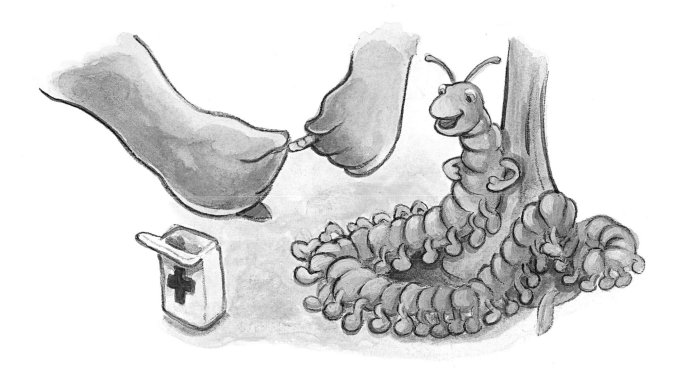

Over the next few days, they would perform many heroic tasks. Two alligators would rush water to a hedgehog with the hiccups, another would apply bandages on the nearly one hundred toes the centipede had stubbed, and all of them would go out of their way to compliment every flamingo in the swamp, telling them that they "looked good in pink," making them blush even pinker!

Even the parrots stopped their repeating when they got their SuperHero Librarian outfits. They stopped repeating everything everyone said and became the best listeners in the swamp. They listened to very quiet whispers in the library.

They listened over swamp tea. They listened when the animals were sad or happy or afraid or just needed a friend.

And the frogs, dressed in their yellow SuperHero Handyman costumes, began using their long tongues to do helpful things—like turning off light switches for animals who couldn't reach them and even retrieving the remote control that had fallen behind the couch for Grandma Rabbit (even if they did get dust bunnies on their tongues in the process).

But no one could believe how much the crabs changed when they got their shocking SuperHero Movie Theater Usher costumes! Those once-bossy crabs now took the lead in helping all the other animals get really good seats at the movie theater.

Chapter Four

Before you knew it—in fact, at super-hero speed—the entire swamp was back to being the very best swamp ever. Everyone was enjoying being a super hero so much that they weren't ready for what happened next.

The SuperHero SuperHero-Maker did a triple somersault and began to fly through the air. All the animals gasped in awe! Until—CRASH! he "flew" into a tree.

(Now, what really happened
was that he tripped on a
leftover ice cream cone
and "fell" through the
air, but the animals
didn't know that.)

Unfortunately, in
crashing through
the tree, a tree
branch caught his
mask and pulled it
off his face. The animals
couldn't believe their eyes.

The SuperHero SuperHero–Maker was no super hero—it was
Ralph the Rabbit!

"You're not a super hero. This is terrible," the animals all cried.

Because as you can guess, if the SuperHero SuperHero–Maker was
not truly a super hero, then he didn't have super hero powers to
make others into super heroes . . . which meant . . . they weren't
really super heroes either!

"Too bad," Alicia Alligator said, "I really liked being a Super-Carer."

"And I liked being a Super-Helper," added Frederick the frog.

"I even liked being a Super-Sharer," admitted Hubba,
the hippo who started the whole mess.

But before everything went back to being terrible, Petunia the Parrot used her super-listener skills, and suggested the animals all listen to what Ralph the Rabbit had to say.

The swamp instantly grew quiet. The crickets stopped chirping, the frogs stopped slurping, and the hippos' ears twitched with hope. Everyone listened.

"You're right. I didn't really make you super heroes. But, don't forget what you started doing when you put on those costumes. The costumes didn't give you powers; they just reminded you of the powers God had given you long ago. I think maybe we really all do have God's power to be super at helping, sharing, listening, and caring—if we'll just try.

Hubba spoke up. "With all of us hogging and snapping, repeating and teasing and bossing each other, things were pretty bad. Ralph the Rabbit helped us remember to treat each other the way God wants us to treat each other— with love and respect. And that's what heroes do!"

After a moment, cheers began to erupt from all over the swamp. Everyone knew that they really were super heroes after all.

"Hey, Ralph, explain something else . . ." Hubba wondered.
"What does the word GMUASH on your super-hero costume mean?"

"God Makes Us All SuperHeroes," Ralph said with a laugh.

And all the animals laughed along with him.

From that moment on,
if alligators seemed snappy,
crabs became bossy, hippos felt hoggy,
or the frogs were tempted to tease,
they would remember GMUASH and the
super strengths inside each of them.

And once again, Super Hero Swamp was the slimiest, stinkiest,
best swamp ever!

Guess what! You can be a super hero too!

Are you a Super-Sharer?
Which super strength has God given you?

A Super-Carer?

A Super-Listener?

A Super-Helper?

A Super-Sharer?

GMUASH!

God Makes Us All SuperHeroes!

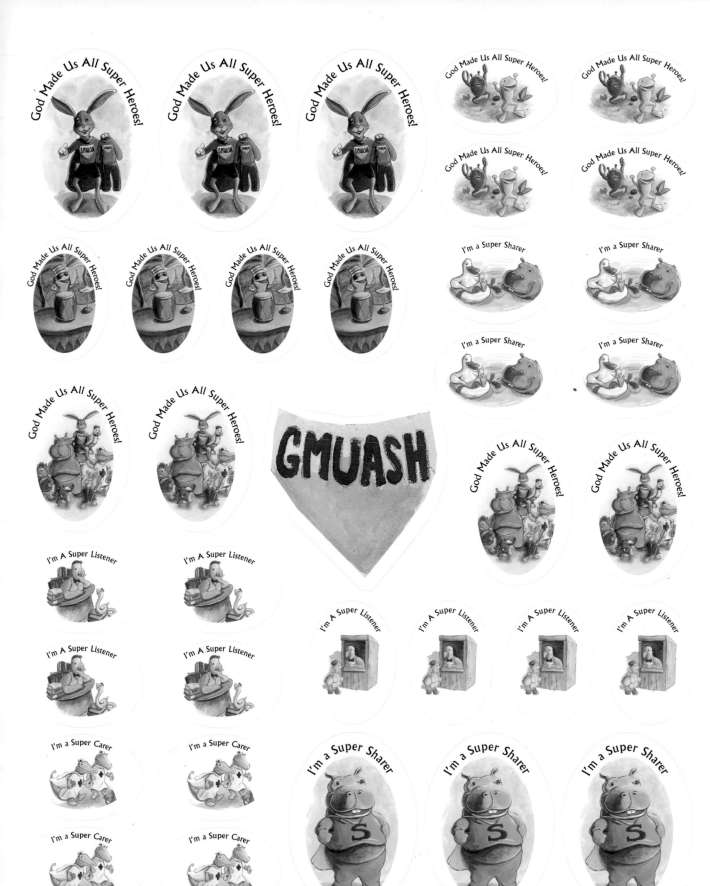

I'm a Super Helper

I'm a Super Helper

I'm a Super Helper

I'm a Super Server

I'm a Super Server

I'm a Super Server

I'm a Super Server

I'm A Super Listener
I'm A Super Listener
I'm A Super Listener
I'm A Super Listener

I'm a Super Carer

I'm a Super Carer

I'm a Super Carer

I'm a Super Carer

God Made Us All Super Heroes!

God Made Us All Super Heroes!

GMUASH

I'm a Super Server

I'm a Super Server

I'm A Super Helper

I'm A Super Helper

I'm A Super Helper

I'm A Super Helper

I'm a Super Server

I'm a Super Server

I'm a Super Server

I'm a Super Server

I'm A Super Helper

I'm A Super Helper

I'm A Super Helper

I'm A Super Helper

I'm a Super Carer

I'm a Super Carer

I'm a Super Carer